S0-CTA-572

CARTOON NETWORK®
SCOOBY-DOO!™
and the
MONSTER BASH
A STORY TOLD IN 3-D

By Jesse Leon McCann

For Nancy Trempe, my chat marathon confidant

ISBN 0-439-31722-3

Illustrated by Duendes del Sur
Designed by Joan Moloney

12 11 10 9 8 7 6 5 4 3 2 1   1 2 3 4 5 6/0
Printed in the U.S.A.
First Scholastic printing, September 2001

SCHOLASTIC INC.
New York   Toronto   London   Auckland   Sydney
Mexico City   New Delhi   Hong Kong   Buenos Aires

Scooby-Doo and the Mystery, Inc. gang had just received a puzzling letter. It said an area near the small town of Fernville was haunted, and it begged them to come help. The letter was unsigned.

On their way to Fernville, the kids stopped for gas and directions. As the attendant helped them, Velma had a funny feeling they were being watched.

Are the kids being spied on? Put on your 3-D glasses and see!

A few miles outside of town, the Mystery Machine got a flat tire. When Fred went to get the spare, it was flat, too!

"It looks like someone's home over there," Daphne said. "Let's ask to use their phone."

"Zoinks!" cried Shaggy. "That place sure looks creepy!"

"Reah, reah! Reepy!" Scooby whimpered.

Velma thought it was odd that both tires were flat. What could have caused it? Put on your 3-D glasses and see if you can find a clue!

When the gang made it to the old mansion, they got a big surprise. A lively Valentine's Day party was in full swing.

"Like, wow, Scooby!" exclaimed Shaggy. "Dig this groovy shindig! They've even got refreshments."

Scooby already knew that. He was over at the goodies table faster than you could say boo!

"Look, it's also a costume party," Daphne observed. "What a clever idea!"

While Fred went looking for a phone, Daphne and Velma mingled with the partygoers. Meanwhile, Shaggy complimented a girl on her witch costume.

"Costume?" the witch replied. She laughed. Then she made a huge fireball appear over Shaggy's head!

"Jinkies!" said Velma nervously. "There's something not quite right here! And I still get the feeling someone's watching us!"

Is Velma right? Put on your 3-D glasses and find out!

Shaggy looked at the smiling witch, then he looked at the other party guests. Then he looked at them even *closer.*

"Zoinks!" Shaggy yelled, running to nab Scooby. "Let's get out of here! Like, these are *real* ghosts and ghoulies!"

"Roh ro!" cried Scooby. He and Shaggy weaved through the monsters and up the stairs.

Just then, a suit of armor came crashing down the stairs toward them. It was like the armor was possessed!

The armor's not haunted, but how did it come loose from the wall? Put on your 3-D glasses and spot the clue!

Shaggy and Scooby dodged the suit of armor and ran into the kitchen. As the others followed, they saw that the kitchen was filled with wildly moving pots and pans!

"Like, monsters in the ballroom and poltergeists in here!" Shaggy bellowed as he ran. "We're doomed!"

"Rooooooh!" yelled Scooby.

"Jeepers, it's like someone's going out of their way to scare us!" Daphne said. "Why would somebody do that?"

"More important, *who* would do that?" asked Velma.

Who indeed? Put on your 3-D glasses. Can you find another clue? What is it?

Shaggy and Scooby fled through the opposite kitchen door, then up another stairway to the second floor. By this time, they were so scared, *everything* frightened them.

"Zoinks! Man, Scooby, we've got to get out of this spooky old house!" Shaggy moaned.

"Ri'm rith roo!" Scooby-Doo agreed. "Ret's ro!"

There's another clue in the creepy hallway. Can you see it? Put on your 3-D glasses and check it out!

Try as they might, Shaggy and Scooby couldn't find a way out of the scary mansion. After stumbling through the top floor of the huge building, they found themselves back where they started — in the ballroom full of monsters!

Worst of all, something tripped them and they went flying over the railing and right toward the surprised monsters! Oh, no!

Were Shaggy and Scooby being clumsy, or did something else trip them? Put on your 3-D glasses and look for a clue!

Luckily, Scooby and Shaggy were able to grab the chandelier in the nick of time!
Instead of falling onto the monsters, they swung themselves back onto the balcony.
Just then, the rest of the kids joined them.
"Come on, gang," Fred said. "We need to find a quiet place to figure out the mystery."
They had to find someplace *fast*! The curious monsters were heading their way!

Scooby and the gang ran into the library. They tried to shut the door, but the monsters tried very hard to get in.

"Hold them back, Shaggy and Scooby!" Velma ordered. "We'll search for another way out."

There weren't any other doors out of the library, just a lot of dusty books and some spooky statues. It looked like they were trapped!

There's something out of place in the library. It's almost as if the gang isn't alone! Slip on your 3-D specs and see!

Then Fred made an amazing discovery — there was an old-fashioned elevator in the library. "Come on, gang!" he called. "Let's get out of here!"

"Like, you don't have to ask me twice," cried Shaggy.

"Ree reither!" Scooby panted.

But as soon as the kids all stepped inside, the elevator went plunging downward! Faster and faster it went!

"Jinkies!" Velma exclaimed. "Someone must have sabotaged it!"

Someone did sabotage the elevator, and left a clue behind!
Use your 3-D glasses to find it!

Just when the kids thought they were going to crash to the ground, they suddenly came to a soft, gentle landing.

Scrambling out of the elevator, they discovered why. A friendly goblin had caught the elevator and set it down carefully, before any damage was done.

"Zoinks! But I thought goblins were people-eating meanies!" Shaggy said.

"Some of us are nice," said the goblin, grinning. "In fact, *all* the monsters at the Valentine's Day bash are nice monsters."

But someone isn't so nice, and that person is hiding in the basement! Grab your 3-D glasses and see if you can spot him!

Suddenly, the goblin reached behind the boxes and pulled somebody out.

"Jinkies! I recognize him from his sign in Fernville!" Velma exclaimed. "It's Ray from Redcoat Realty!"

"He's been trying to get rid of us since he opened his office," explained the witch. "He doesn't think he can sell property with us living around here."

"You can't prove I did anything!" snarled Ray.

But some items fell from Ray's pocket that tied him to the other clues! With your 3-D glasses, you can see that clearly!

"Ray sent that mysterious letter," Fred explained. "Then he tried to scare us into thinking this area was haunted."

"He wanted us to expose the monsters and drive them away," Velma added.

"But, like, it looks like his plan backfired!" Shaggy laughed.

"Oh, is this the famous monster mansion?" asked one man. "I can't wait to buy a home in such an interesting neighborhood!"

As the police led him away, Ray grumbled, "I never should have gotten involved with those meddling kids and their dog!"

The Mystery, Inc. kids went back inside the monster mansion and rejoined the bash. Now everybody had something extra to celebrate! Ray had been exposed, the monsters could live near Fernville in peace, and the gang had solved another mystery!

(And you helped, too, with your 3-D glasses!)

"Like, last but not least, we made some new friends and have a whole bunch of snacks to eat, too!" Shaggy grinned. "Right, Scoob?"

All Scooby could do was cheer, "Scooby-Dooby-Doo!"